Y0-CAZ-625

Cuddle Bunny

BY CHARLES GHIGNA
ILLUSTRATED BY JACQUELINE EAST

PICTURE WINDOW BOOKS
a capstone imprint

WEST HARTFORD
2813
PUBLIC LIBRARY

For Charlotte Rose

Tiny Tales are published by Picture Window Books,
a Capstone imprint
1710 Roe Crest Drive
North Mankato, Minnesota 56003
www.capstonepub.com

Copyright © 2016 by Picture Window Books, a Capstone imprint

All rights reserved. No part of this publication may be reproduced
in whole or in part, or stored in a retrieval system, or transmitted in
any form or by any means, electronic, mechanical, photocopying,
recording, or otherwise, without written permission of the publisher.

Library of Congress Cataloging-in-Publication Data
Ghigna, Charles, author. Cuddle Bunny / by Charles Ghigna ;
illustrated by Jacqueline East.
pages cm -- (Tiny tales)

Summary: In four simple stories, a young bunny named Cuddle
learns to appreciate herself, enjoys reading to her friends, finding a
message in a bottle, and plays pirate.

ISBN 978-1-4795-6528-3 (library binding)
ISBN 978-1-4795-6532-0 (paperback.)
ISBN 978-1-4795-8479-6 (eBook)

1. Rabbits--Juvenile fiction. 2. Animals--Juvenile fiction. 3.
Conduct of life--Juvenile fiction. [1. Rabbits--Fiction. 2. Animals--
Fiction. 3. Conduct of life--Fiction.] I. East, Jacqueline, illustrator.
II. Title.

PZ7.G3390234Cu 2016
[E]--dc23   2014045631

Designer: Kristi Carlson

Printed in the United States of America in Stevens Point, Wisconsin.
032015   008824WZF15

J
GHIGNA   11.22
CHARLES

table of contents

1

Every Bunny's Different

One morning, Cuddle Bunny looked at herself in the mirror. She was not happy.

"My teeth are too big," she said.

Cuddle Bunny looked in the mirror again.

"My ears are too big, too," she said.

Cuddle Bunny slowly hopped downstairs. She sat at the kitchen table. She didn't touch her breakfast.

"What's the matter, my little bunny?" asked her mother.

"Nothing," said Cuddle Bunny.

"Well, nothing must be something if it makes you look this sad," said her father.

Cuddle Bunny was quiet. Then she stared down at her plate.

"My teeth are too big," she said.

"Your teeth are bright and white," said her father.

"They are just right for you," said her mother.

"Well, my ears are too big, too," said Cuddle Bunny.

"Your ears are pink and perfect," said her father.

"They are just right for you," said her mother.

"They look too big," said Cuddle Bunny.

"Your cousin Jack has ears and teeth that are much bigger than yours," said her father.

"Yes, and they are just right for him," said her mother.

"You're right," said Cuddle Bunny.

"Your cousin Angela has small ears and long fur," said her father.

"And they are just right for her," said her mother.

"Your cousin Holly has ears that hang down on either side of her face," said her father.

"I know, I know," said Cuddle Bunny. "And they are just right for her."

"Every bunny is different. That's what makes each of us so special," her mother said.

"You have to say that because you are my mom," said Cuddle Bunny.

Her mother laughed.

"Well, how boring would it be if we all looked alike?" her mother said.

"I guess it would be pretty boring," Cuddle Bunny said, smiling. "And a little weird."

"It sure would," her mother said. "It's important to be the best you that you can be."

"And it doesn't matter what you look like," her father said. "However, not every bunny looks different."

"Yes, they do," her mother said.

"What about twins?" Cuddle Bunny asked.

"Okay, okay," her mother said. "Some bunnies do look alike."

"I'm not talking about twins," her father said.

He got up from the kitchen table and hopped to the living room. He returned with an old photo album.

"Look," he said, pointing at one of the pictures. "Do you see that little bunny in the picture?"

"She looks just like me!" said Cuddle Bunny.

"Yes, she does," he said.

"Who is that little bunny?" asked Cuddle Bunny.

"That is your mother when she was your age," said her father.

"Wow!" said Cuddle Bunny.

"Wow!" said her mother.

Cuddle Bunny smiled at her mother. Her mother smiled back.

"We love your pink cheeks and little fluffy tail," said her mother.

"And your white teeth and pink ears," said her father.

"But most of all, we love YOU and all the little things that make you YOU," said her mother.

"We sure do," said her father. "Every bunny's different. And we are so glad you are our one and only Cuddle Bunny."

"Me too," said Cuddle Bunny. "Me too."

2

Cuddle Bunny Tells a Story

Cuddle Bunny sat back on her bed with her friends. It was story time! Her animal friends were ready. She read to them every night.

"What story are we going to hear tonight?" asked Teddy Bear.

"I hope it's about a princess," said Pink Pony.

"Does it have a jungle in it?" asked Sock Monkey.

"A jungle with lots of bamboo would be great," said Anna Panda.

"Amazing!" said Cuddle Bunny. "You guessed it."

"Really?" Pink Pony asked.

"You sure did. This is a story about a princess who gets lost in a bamboo jungle," Cuddle Bunny said.

"How exciting!" everyone said.

"Is everyone ready?" Cuddle Bunny asked.

"Yes!" they all said.

"Once upon a time, there lived a beautiful princess," Cuddle Bunny began, looking at all of her friends.

"Each day she went to her castle window. She looked out at the big jungle of bamboo," she said.

"I love bamboo," said Anna Panda.

Cuddle Bunny smiled and kept talking. "The princess wondered what it would be like to go out into that jungle. She had heard there was a land of stuffed animals. The animals loved books and met each night to hear a new story."

"That sounds like us," said Teddy Bear.

"Yes, it does," said Sock Monkey.

"Go on! Go on!" said Pink Pony.
"What happens next?"

"One early morning, the princess tiptoed to the castle door. She opened it slowly and quietly. Then she ran down the path toward the bamboo jungle."

Cuddle Bunny paused.

"What? What happens next?" asked Teddy Bear.

"Where did she go?" asked Pink Pony.

"What did she see?" asked Sock Monkey.

"Who did she meet?" asked Anna Panda.

Cuddle Bunny smiled. "Well, she walked through the forest until she came to a creek. An old wooden bridge was over the creek. It led to the other side of the jungle. Do you think she crossed the bridge?"

"Yes!" her friends shouted.

"You are right. And when she did, the princess realized she was lost. She was afraid," Cuddle Bunny said.

Then she paused again.

"Don't stop! Don't stop!" said her animal friends.

"On the other side of the jungle, she saw four friendly animals," Cuddle Bunny said.

"Who? Who? Who were the animals?" they all asked.

"A bear, a pony, a monkey, and a panda," she said.

"What were their names?" Anna Panda asked.

"Teddy, Pink, Sock, and Anna," Cuddle Bunny said, laughing.

"Those are some great names," said Anna Panda.

"Very funny," said Teddy Bear, laughing.

"Oh, Cuddle Bunny," said Pink Pony.

"Cuddle Bunny likes reading to us each night," said Anna Panda.

"But she likes making up her own stories even more!" said Sock Monkey.

"I sure do," said Cuddle Bunny.

A Message in a Bottle

It was a sunny afternoon at the beach. Cuddle Bunny and her parents put their blanket on the warm sand. Her father set up a big umbrella for shade.

Then they hopped down to the water. They looked out at the sea. It was a perfect summer day.

A little wave rolled in. It washed over Cuddle Bunny's feet. She laughed. The water tickled her toes. She waited and watched for the next wave to come.

Just as the wave was about to touch her toes, she hopped back. When the wave headed back out to sea, she hopped after it. As another wave came washing up, Cuddle Bunny turned and hopped back, giggling.

"Look!" she said. "The waves are playing tag with me!"

Cuddle Bunny's parents laughed.

As she and her parents were heading back to their blanket, Cuddle Bunny saw something in the water.

"Look!" said Cuddle Bunny as she pointed to the green bottle.

The wave brought the bottle to the shore. Cuddle Bunny's father picked it up.

"There's a note inside," he said.

"A message in a bottle! How exciting," her mother said.

"What does it say?" asked Cuddle Bunny.

"Let's have a look," he said as they headed back to their blanket.

Cuddle Bunny's father pulled the cork out of the bottle. Then he turned the bottle upside down. A rolled-up piece of paper fell out.

"Can I read it?" asked Cuddle Bunny.

"Sure," her father said. He gave her the paper.

Cuddle Bunny slowly unrolled it. She did not want the note to rip.

"Oh, no! I can't read this," Cuddle Bunny said. She gave the note to her mother.

"It's in Spanish," her mother said.

"What does it say?" Cuddle Bunny asked.

"It says, 'Hello! My name is Maria. I live in Mexico. May the sea carry my letter to you.'"

"Did that bottle come from Mexico?" asked Cuddle Bunny.

"It did," said her mother.

"That is so cool!" said Cuddle Bunny. "Can we write a message?"

"We sure can," said her mother. "What would you like to say?"

"Let's say, 'Hello! My name is Cuddle Bunny. I live in the United States. May the sea carry my letter to you.'"

"Perfect," her mother said.

"We can write your note on the same paper. Then the next person to find the bottle can read both of the notes," her father said.

"That's a great idea!" said Cuddle Bunny.

"We can put the bottle back in the sea. The waves will carry the bottle away. When someone else finds it, they can add their name to the note and send it back out again," her mother said.

Cuddle Bunny and her parents hopped back to the water. Her father rolled up the paper with the messages on it. Then he tucked it back into the bottle. He put the cork back in the bottle. Then he handed the bottle to Cuddle Bunny.

She waited for a big wave to wash up on the shore. Just as it was about to roll back out, Cuddle Bunny tossed the bottle into the water. She watched it bob up and down as it floated away.

"Goodbye," said Cuddle Bunny, waving.

That night, Cuddle Bunny fell asleep thinking about her day at the beach. She thought about the bottle that had traveled from Mexico. She wondered how far it would travel with her new message inside.

Cuddle Bunny dreamed that some day she would travel the world like that beautiful green bottle.

The Pirate Ship

Cuddle Bunny jumped out of bed. She grabbed her pirate hat and hopped downstairs.

"Good morning, Captain," said her mother.

"Ahoy," said Cuddle Bunny. "What's the grub?"

"Pancakes and bacon," said her mother.

"Aye," said Cuddle Bunny. "What's to drink?"

"Chocolate milk," said her mother.

"Thanks, Mate," Cuddle Bunny said.

After breakfast, Cuddle Bunny
pulled her wagon down the sidewalk.
She was looking for treasure.

She saw a huge box next to a
trash can. The box was the perfect
size for a pirate ship.

"It's me lucky day," said Cuddle Bunny. She loaded the box onto her wagon. Then she headed back home to set up her pirate ship.

Cuddle Bunny needed supplies. She found her crayons, markers, scissors, and paper. She also found her telescope.

Cuddle Bunny spent the morning making her pirate ship. She even made her own pirate flag.

Her mother brought out sandwiches
and juice for lunch. They had a picnic
in the pirate ship.

"I can't wait to show Dad my ship.
I'll make him my first mate," said
Cuddle Bunny.

Cuddle Bunny played in the pirate ship all afternoon. She napped and ate dinner in her ship. She was looking out one of the portholes as her father drove up.

"Ahoy, Mate!" said Cuddle Bunny.

"Yo-ho-ho!" replied her father.

Cuddle Bunny noticed her dad carrying a covered cage.

"What's that?" asked Cuddle Bunny.

"A gift for my favorite pirate," said her dad. He pulled the cover off.

Cuddle Bunny couldn't believe her eyes! It was a parrot! It was bright blue and red, and it could talk!

"Yo-ho-ho!" said the parrot.

"Yo-ho-ho!" said Cuddle Bunny.

"Let's give him a name," said her
father, smiling.

"Great idea!" said Cuddle Bunny.

"The only pirate names I know are Black Beard, Blue Beard, and Red Beard," said her father.

"I like Blue Beard best," said Cuddle Bunny.

"Perfect!" said her father.

Cuddle Bunny turned to her parrot. "You are Pirate Blue Beard."

"Yo-ho-ho!" said the parrot.

It was getting late, and Cuddle Bunny was getting sleepy.

"What do you say we camp out in your ship tonight?" asked her father.

"Aye aye, Mate," said Cuddle Bunny.

Her father went in the house. He came back with sleeping bags, a flashlight, and chocolate chip cookies.

They ate the cookies and talked. Then they climbed into their sleeping bags.

"Good night, Captain," said her dad.

"Good night, Mate," said Captain Cuddle Bunny.

"Good night," said Pirate Blue Beard.

Glossary

bamboo (bam-BOO) — a tropical plant that has a hard, hollow stem often used for making furniture

camp (KAMP) — to live and sleep outdoors for a little while, usually in tents or in cabins

cork (KORK) — a stopper used to plug a bottle

creek (KREEK) — a stream of water that's smaller than a river

grub (GRUHB) — food

picnic (PIK-nik) — a party or trip that includes eating a meal or snacks outdoors

portholes (PORT-hohlz) — small, round windows on the side of a boat or ship realized (REE-ul-lahyzd) — became aware of something

shore (SHOR) — the land along the edge of a river, pond, lake, sea, or ocean

special (SPESH-uhl) — different from what is usual

telescope (TEL-uh-skohp) — an instrument that makes objects that are far away seem larger and close

tiptoed (TIP-tohd) — walked very quietly on or as if you were on the tips of your toes

Discussion Questions

1. Cuddle Bunny told an exciting story to her stuffed animals about a princess in a bamboo jungle. Tell a story to your friends or stuffed animals.

2. The message in the bottle floated all the way from Mexico to the United States. That's a long way! If you could go anywhere in the world, where would you go?

3. Cuddle Bunny pretended she was a pirate. When you play pretend, what do you pretend to be?

4. Mom and Dad did a lot of nice things for Cuddle Bunny. They took her to the beach, they made her cookies, and they gave her a parrot. Talk about the nice things that your parents do for you.

5. Cuddle Bunny had fun playing on the beach. Talk about a fun place where you like to go to play.

6. At first, Cuddle Bunny was sad because she didn't like the way she looked. But her parents helped to cheer her up. What things make you feel happy when you are feeling sad?

Writing Prompts

1. Cuddle Bunny likes pirates. Write a story about a pirate who has adventures on the sea.

2. Draw a picture of your favorite stuffed animal, and write a paragraph that describes why it is your favorite.

3. Cuddle Bunny found a message in a bottle from a girl in Mexico. Write your own message in a bottle.

4. Cuddle Bunny's white teeth and pink ears are just right for her. They make her special. Write a list of what makes you special.

5. Dad and Mom surprised Cuddle Bunny by giving her a pet parrot. Write about an animal that you would really like to have as a pet. Why would it make a good pet?

6. Cuddle Bunny added her animal friends into her story. Write your own story about you and your friends going on adventure.

Author Bio

Charles Ghigna (also known as Father Goose®) lives in a tree house in Alabama. He is the author of more than 100 award-winning books for children and adults from Random House, Capstone, Disney, Hyperion, Scholastic, Simon & Schuster, Abrams, Charlesbridge, and other publishers.

His poems appear in hundreds of magazines, from *The New Yorker* and *Harper's* to *Cricket* and *Highlights*. He is a former poetry editor of the *English Journal* and nationally syndicated feature writer for Tribune Media Services.

Illustrator Bio

Jacqueline East has been illustrating children's books for many years. Her work has been published across the globe and is known for its warm innocence and humor. Everything is an inspiration, and she especially loves the golden atmosphere of twilight; a magical time of day that is often the backdrop for her characters.

She has worked above a chocolate factory, in a caravan by the sea, and now, from her home in Bristol with Scampi the dog sleeping in the corner of the studio!